HEAD SMASHED IN
A Short Story

W. Fred Bowen

Illustrated by
Rosauro Ugang

Copyright © 2011 by W. Fred Bowen. 87685-BOWE
Library of Congress Control Number: 2011902444

ISBN:
Softcover   978-1-4568-7033-1
Hardcover   978-1-4568-7034-8

All rights reserved. No part of this book may be reproduced
or transmitted in any form or by any means, electronic or
mechanical, including photocopying, recording, or by any
information storage and retrieval system, without permission
in writing from the copyright owner.

This is a work of fiction. Names, characters, places and incidents
either are the product of the author's imagination or are used
fictitiously, and any resemblance to any actualpersons, living or
dead, events, or locales is entirely coincidental.

This book was printed in the United States of America.

To order additional copies of this book, contact:
Xlibris Corporation
1-888-795-4274
www.Xlibris.com
Orders@Xlibris.com

To My Sons

Greg & Josh

To remind you of those thrilling days of yesteryear, slogging through

dirt, dust, sand and wind and stumbling on treasures.

John and Shelly —
This is one of my
passions —
Wfred Bower

FORWARD

The short story before you is a work of fiction. It is not intended to be a definition for the naming of the area where it takes place. Instead, it is a reminder to me of the rewarding years I spent living in the Canadian Province of Alberta and exploring its many interesting and exciting historic and pre-historic locations.

For years, long before Head Smashed In Buffalo Jump became a World Heritage Site, I frequently spent Sunday afternoons walking the kill site, exploring the drive lines and campsites, and just sitting and thinking. It was, at that time, my most favourite location in the world — a place where I was able to find 'thinking' space. In those days which are already becoming a part of history, I was fascinated by the images that came to mind while exploring there. The sounds, sights and smells of the great buffalo herds, the panic and confusion which must have prevailed and the exuberating shouts and actions of the indigenous people intrigued and inspired me. I would so have given anything to be able to travel back in time to observe one of the great hunts that transpired in this place.

Unfortunately, no one is alive today who experienced firsthand the excitement and drama of a real buffalo drive. It would be all too sad if the history of this site and many more like it were to disappear forever. It is for this reason that I determined to write a story which would capture my ideas about what must have occurred there and which would give others some insight into what it may have been like.

The spear point described in the story is based on an actual type of tool (called an Eden Point) which has been found occasionally on the prairies of Alberta. While such weapons were not used in the buffalo jumps, nevertheless, early people had used them to kill the animals they utilised as food. Eden Points are at least 10,000 years old and predate, therefore, the killing of large numbers of animals in kill sites such as Head Smashed In Buffalo Jump. It is obvious that more recent native people on the prairies found such items as they wandered the land in search of sustenance, and it has been recorded that they attributed such tools to "little people", the subject of many of their legends.

And just a word about the winds of southern Alberta; anyone who has spent any time there at all knows that the winds blow long and hard. They are characteristic of the land and its forms and have had a tremendous impact on the life, not only of the aboriginals, but also of the people living there today. A respect and admiration for these winds is difficult to foster, but Alberta would not be the beautiful land it is today without them. Long may they blow.

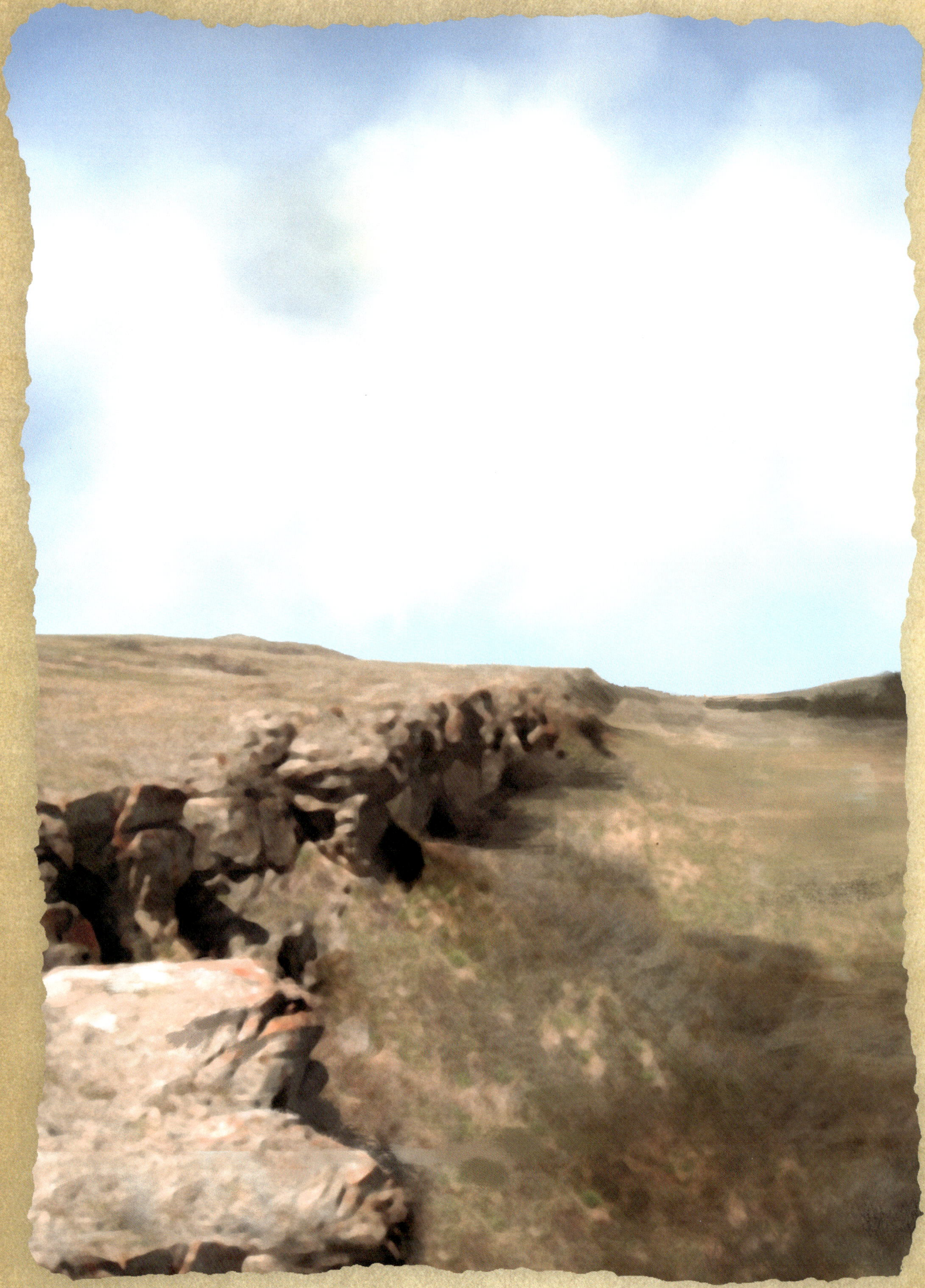

CHAPTER 1

For nearly an hour before his dad came downstairs to wake him, Mike heard the wind. Lying there in his bed, he imagined the wind whipping across the prairies from the foothills to the west, blowing the grasses so they looked like waves on the sea. In southern Alberta the wind seemed to be almost alive—at least in Mike's mind. It was born somewhere up on the slopes of the Rocky Mountains where there was still snow in the ravines and where dark, misty clouds covered the high ground. It gained momentum as it travelled down the mountains, brushing the evergreen forests and growing stronger with each contact. Leaving the mountains and crossing the grass-covered foothills, the wind gained a momentum which would carry it hundreds of miles before it would begin to die—truly a life of its own.

"Mike, come alive, son!" Mike felt a gentle pressure on his shoulder. "Whoops, I must have fallen asleep again," blustered Mike. And then he remembered—it was morning and time to go. He leaped out of bed and pulled on his jeans. "Put on your long-johns, Mike," his dad called from upstairs. "The wind is really whipping out there."

When Mike climbed the stairs to the kitchen, breakfast was already on the table. Cheese-covered bacon, fried hard and crisp in a hot pan the way only his dad could do it, eggs, toast and milk were ready to be devoured. Mike loved to eat breakfast when his dad prepared it—not because it tasted much differently, but because his dad prepared it. "Eat as much as you can, son. We probably won't eat again until late this afternoon. The wind is blowing just hard enough for this to be a perfect day."

Mike glanced out the kitchen window. With the sun just beginning to light up the western clouds, he could see the Chinook arch distinctly on the horizon. The west wind was pushing the clouds ahead of it, causing an end-of-the-tunnel effect in the sky. Mike began to feel a tickle of excitement deep in his stomach—right under the bacon and eggs.

A murmured "Goodbye and good luck!" came from the upstairs bedroom—mom was still in bed—and Mike headed out the door. As he walked out of the house, the wind nearly blew him over. With great anticipation he climbed into the Volkswagen Beetle and was quickly joined by his dad; they were soon on the street heading out of town.

"Which way are we headed, dad?" asked Mike. "Along the Old Man River—that spot where the Little Bow flows into the Old Man should be reasonably good on a morning like this. I understand the sandy soil in that area has really been blowing for the past couple of weeks."

Mike knew his father was as excited as he was. They had been hunting arrowheads as long as Mike could remember and dad had been hunting them since he was a boy. Their collection was already large, but the thrill of finding more artefacts never seemed to lessen—in fact, it seemed to Mike that it got more and more exciting.

Spring in southern Alberta, before it was warm and dry enough for farmers to work the fields was the best time to go looking. The furious west wind seemed to delight in blowing the light top-soil away. No matter what the farmers did to prevent this erosion, the spring winds always played havoc in hundreds of locations.

"Keep your eyes peeled for blowing dirt, Mike. We'll try to look in all of the places we can find." Mike nodded his head, yawned because of the heat thrown out by the heater, and stared steadily out the window. Fifteen minutes later, Mike yelled, "Look at that cloud of dust!" The Volkswagen pulled slowly to the edge of the gravel road. "This looks like a pretty good spot," said his dad. "The dirt along the top of that small rise is blowing. Let's go up and take a look."

As Mike held up the middle wire of the barbed wire fence with his hand, his foot pushing down on the bottom wire so his dad could climb through, he noticed the sun shining brightly on the horizon. Even though the wind was gusting like crazy, it was going to be a warm day. As they walked through the stubble field, the dry stalks cracked and popped against their legs. Suddenly, WHIRRR, WHOOSH and a bevy of Hungarian Partridge flew protesting away from their morning meal. Mike grinned to himself, "That's a good sign—this is going to be a fantastic day!"

When they finally reached the bare earth between the strips of stubble, the blowing dirt immediately assaulted Mike's eyes and nose. "Keep your head turned away from the wind, Mike.

Otherwise you'll be eating a second breakfast made out of mud." Mike smiled and started looking closely at the ground. Walking slowly, with his back to the wind, his eyes searched the bare patches of dirt ahead and to the sides. His dad had moved off to the other side of the ploughed area and Mike knew they would cover the entire area, walking slowly back and forth in straight lines, from one side of the bare patch to the other.

With dirt constantly blowing into his face, Mike found it hard to concentrate. "Hey! I've got one!" dad yelled. Mike knew he shouldn't run over to where dad was standing because he might miss something, but after scraping his boot in the dirt to make a mark he could return to, he ran to his dad's side. "Let's see it! Is it a big one?" Dad held out the palm of his hand; a perfectly shaped point about three centimetres long with side notches lay in his hand. It was beautifully flaked and was brown. Mike immediately recognized the material as Knife River flint and knew that it was not common to Alberta, but that it came from a location in North Dakota, across the border in the United States.

With obvious envy Mike said, "That's a dandy, dad. I hope there are more here." "Where there's one, there's always more. Let's find them!" said his dad and once again began his slow walk.

Mike watched his father walk away and smiled. He looked so serious in a funny sort of way, walking with his hands in the pockets of his jacket and his head tilted forward, eyes on the ground. The slow, shuffling steps made him look like a man lost in deep thought. Mike laughed a little when he thought of cars passing by; they always slowed down a little bit to see this strange walk out in the middle of a dirt field. "They must make some strange comments when they see us," thought Mike. Mike returned to his mark in the dirt, put his head down, his hands going behind his back and began to walk carefully across the field.

Thirty minutes later, back in the car, Mike studied the fruits of their labour. There wasn't much. Dad had found the single perfect arrowhead, two turtleback thumb scrapers and some flint flakes. Mike had found the broken tip of an arrowhead and nothing else. "Well, there wasn't much there, Mike. But if the wind keeps blowing like this we should come back here in a few days and check this spot again." Dad wrote down the location in his little notebook and they were on their way again. By noon they had made three other stops, but had found very little else. The only exciting find was a complete hammer head—a large piece of granite about the size of Mike's two fists, with a perfect groove around the middle. Mike knew the people who had left it there hundreds of years earlier had attached a wooden or bone handle to it, using leather straps fitted into the groove. These maul-shaped hammers had many uses around the camp, from pounding stakes into the ground around the tepees, to breaking bones of animals in order to get at the rich marrow within. Mike's dad said, "There are undoubtedly tens of thousands of these stones lying in fields across Canada. Many of them have been picked up by farmers in years gone by and you can often find them in the rock piles near the edges of cultivated fields. Farmers often use them as door stops for their screen doors too, or to adorn their flower beds." Mike had found a broken one the previous year down by the St. Mary's River and hoped to find a perfect one someday.

Riding along in the car, Mike knew his dad was disappointed. They would have to be heading home soon and they really hadn't found very much. Mike felt the same—probably worse. Dad had at least found a couple of nice pieces—all he had found was one broken tip. What a disappointing day this had turned out to be. Mike would like nothing better than to find something really extraordinary, something his dad would also be excited about.

"Well, we had better head 'er home, son. Your mother is expecting us before dark." Mike's dad turned the VW around and headed back towards the city.

Mike was severely disappointed. He loved hunting arrowheads, but it wasn't all that much fun when he found almost nothing. Secretly he had always hoped to fine one piece which would be the prize of their collection...something big and beautiful which would catch everyone's eye when displayed. And way down deep inside he knew that this something would be better than anything his dad had ever found. If only. . .

As they approached the bridge across the Old Man River, Mike's dad said, "Look over there . . . on top of the bluff. Do you see the dirt blowing? I think there might be a good blowout up there. We still have time to check it out." With that, he pulled the car to the shoulder of the gravel road and parked. "Let's go!"

Mike climbed slowly out of the car. "It'll just be another wild goose chase," he thought to himself. "And this time we have to climb clear to the top of the bluff to look at it. Oh, well. . ."

The sun had become very warm for this time of year. Mike felt like shedding his jacket, but thought better of it because of the ferocious wind which they would encounter at the top of the bluff. Both of them were puffing like steam engines when they reached the prairie at the top of the river bank. Looking back at the VW, Mike was surprised to realize how far they had

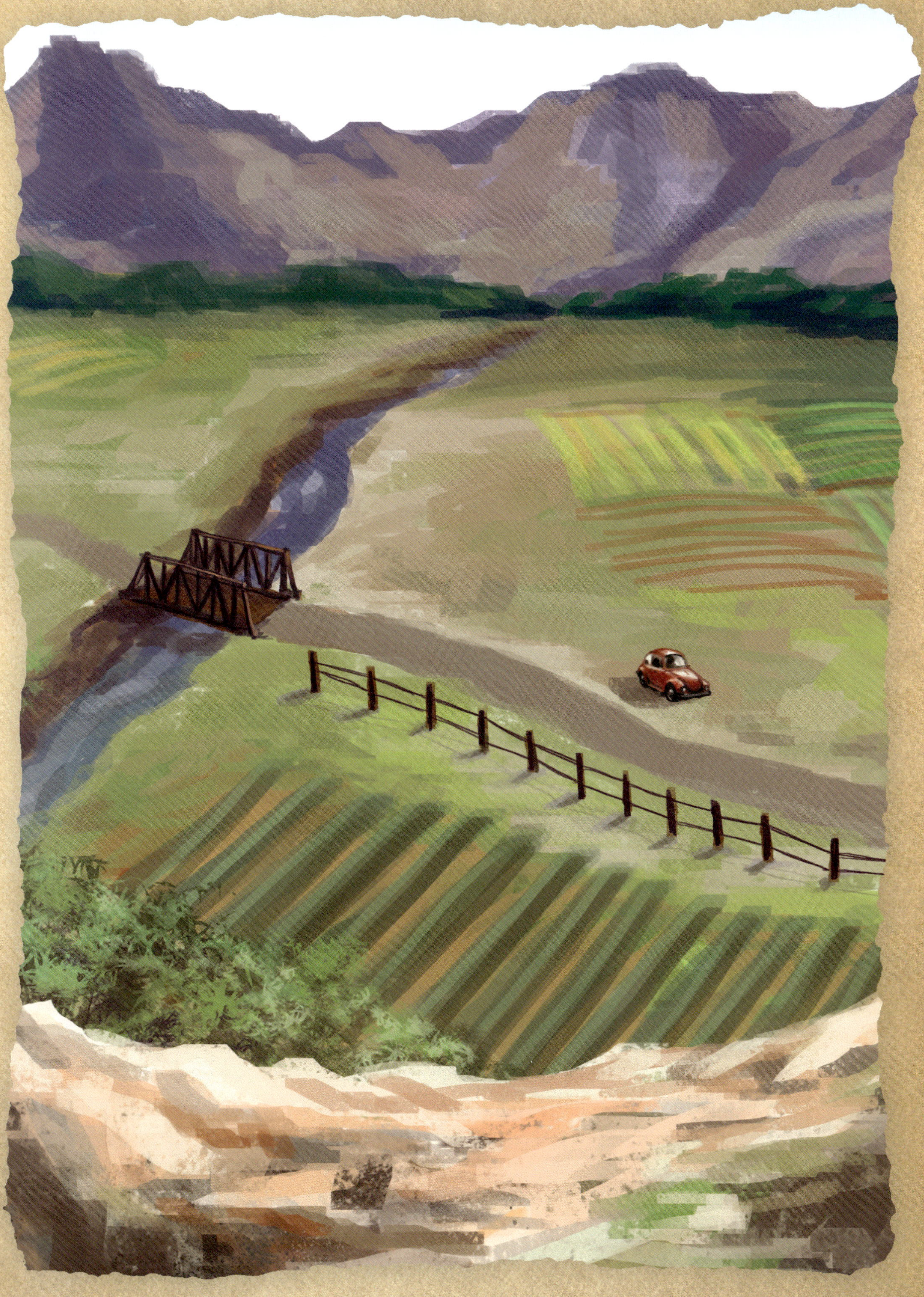

climbed—it looked like a toy parked beside the road.

The west wind was gusting strongly at the top; when Mike realized how large the blown out area was, he was surprised. The edge of the field along the rim of the river bank had been blown away right down to the hardpan and was the length of a city block. The width varied from about two meters to six and the large blown out area was nearly a meter deep. It looked promising.

"I'll start here. You go down to the other end and we'll work towards the center," said Mike's dad. "OK," said Mike and as he walked away, he muttered to himself, "Here we go again." He had only taken a few steps when his dad yelled, "Here's a small obsidian point! This spot could be great!"

Mike reached the other end of the blowout and stated his slow shuffle back across the rock-hard soil. Immediately he noticed small bone flakes scattered about. "Well, what do you know—buffalo bone. That's a good sign at least," he thought to himself. He slowed his step to be sure he didn't miss anything. Reaching down, he picked up a piece of bone to study more closely. It somehow didn't look quite like the buffalo bone he was used to finding. Then, out of the corner of his eye, he saw a small round piece of bone with a hole through it. "Hey!" he said out loud, "that's a bone bead!" He picked it up and turned it over and over in his hand. "I wonder where this came from."

Walking even more slowly now, Mike saw pieces of rock lying scattered around the ground. He immediately recognized them as hearth stones, or as his dad often called them, ". . . fire broken rock". Some fragments were large and some small and they were all a pale red color. Mike knew the color was the result of their contact with fire a long time ago. His dad had told him that they were often heated in the campfire and then dropped red hot into whatever was being cooked.

Mike began to feel a ticklish sensation in his stomach. Sensing an exciting discovery, he knelt down on his hands and knees and crawled slowly along, searching each centimeter of ground around him. Sticking straight up out of the dirt right in front of his nose, Mike saw a sharp point. Carefully brushing away the light, loose soil, a beautiful white arrow point came into view. Mike picked it up and examined it closely. It was perfect!

"Dad! Dad!" he yelled. "You'd better come here. I've found some things!" His dad's head snapped up and he looked in Mike's direction with a questioning look on his face. Mike knew his dad hadn't heard him clearly because of the gusting wind, but by the way he was looking he must have detected the excitement in Mike's voice. "What have you got?" his father shouted. Mike heard him plainly because his voice traveled with the wind. Instead of answering, however, Mike just waved his hand indicating that his dad should come to him.

Just as his father reached his side, Mike found another bead. "What 'cha got there?" asked his dad, somewhat out of breath—he had come running. Mike proudly showed him the point and the two beads and then pointed out the bone and rock fragments in the dirt. "What do you think, dad? Neat, eh?" Mike blurted out. Turning the objects over and over in his hand, Mike's dad let out a low whistle. "Do you know what you've found here?" he said, picking up a piece of bone from the dirt. "This isn't buffalo bone. This is human bone. Sometime a long time ago an Indian died and was left here on top of this ridge. The beads are here because the dead warrior was dressed in his best clothes. He was likely wrapped in a buffalo robe and placed here together with his weapons, to begin his journey into the next life, according to his beliefs. I'll bet if we look more closely, we'll find more pieces."

With that, Mike and his dad began to search the area even more carefully. Both of them were on their hands and knees exploring carefully the exposed area. Occasionally, one of them would emit a sharp cry or an excited shout and then quickly pick up an item from the ground. After about fifteen minutes of this, they had searched the immediate area thoroughly. They laid their finds in the dirt to study them. When they were lined up on the ground, the finds were impressive. There were thirteen bone beads, six complete arrow points and nine grizzly bear claws, each with a perfectly round hole through the rounded end. Mike and his father were quiet as they stared at this impressive array. Finding so many pieces in one location was absolutely amazing. Though none of the pieces contemplated by itself would have been too exceptional, the total group was overwhelming.

Mike was enjoying his feelings of excitement. He was extremely happy that he had been the one to stumble on these amazing artefacts. However, deep inside he felt a slight disappointment because he hadn't found that elusive item he longed for—an artefact that would stand out from all the rest in their collection. "Oh, well," he thought, "maybe something like that just doesn't exist anymore."

"Hey, Mike, that is really something," his father said finally, indicating the items spread out before them. "It makes one wonder who the last person to hold and look at these things was, doesn't it?" Mike nodded and said, "Yes, it would be great if we could learn where these pieces came from. I'll bet there is a super story here."

The west wind continued to gust around them and the loose soil was already beginning to cover over some of their finds. Mike and his dad scooped the pieces up and put them in their pockets, making sure they were deep and carefully placed so they would not be lost or broken. Mike looked up and saw his father had turned, looking over the rim of the bank down into the bottom toward the river. He turned his gaze in the same direction and looked.

The river flowed slowly along, rocks sticking out of the water here and there, creating v-shaped riffles behind them. Small waves seemed to blow over the surface of the water as the wind gusted. Along the bank of the river, which was more than a meter above the water level, the short prairie grasses too were moving wave-like as the wind passed over them. To the left, about ninety meters downstream, thick bushes, "buck brush", grew from a small ravine. The brush was bare of leaves, but appeared a dark maroon color and was moving vigorously in the wind. Upstream to the right, perhaps two hundred meters and just on this side of the bridge stood several cottonwood trees. Many of the trees were young and appeared as small poles stuck in the ground. Five old, large cottonwoods stood in the middle of the smaller trees. Their branches created inter-twining, criss-crossing patterns in the spring sky and it was impossible to tell where one tree began, ended and where another began. Below the trees and inter-laced between the smaller branches were bunches of silvery, gray-colour brush and deadfall. Autumn's leaves were still to be seen scattered everywhere on the ground between the trees and brush.

Mike's mind was deeply engrossed in this picture when his father suddenly said, "I'll bet the family of the man who died was camped there beside the trees. There is plenty of fire-wood there and easy access to the water in the river."

Mike pointed his head in that direction. "Do you think we could find anything down there?" "Oh, I doubt it," said his dad. "It was likely a very small camp and without any kind of erosion, any remains are buried deep beneath the surface of the ground. But they sure couldn't have found a more beautiful place to set up their camp."

For several minutes more, Mike and his father remained there, looking over and enjoying the serenity of the area. The only sounds to disturb the scene were the moans, whistles and rustles of the wind. It was almost as if nature recognized the sadness discovered by Mike and his dad and was in sympathy with their thoughts. "Well, son, let's go home. We can cover the rest of this blowout on our way. You move over to the far edge and I'll walk along here." Mike turned into the wind and began to walk to the far side of the blown-out area. He had taken no more than two steps, one of them over a clump of grass still growing in the sifting soil when he saw it. Just behind the clump a shiny glint indicated flint. Stopping and turning his back to the wind, he looked directly behind the grass. His breath came out in a rush. He blinked his eyes—once, twice— to be sure he wasn't seeing things. Falling to his knees, he continued to stare in utter amazement. His dad, just a short distance away, had seen him drop down. He squinted into the wind in order to see what was going on. Mike didn't look up; he didn't call out, he didn't move.

"What do you see, son?" his father yelled into the wind. There was still no movement, no sound and absolutely no response. Seconds later, Mike's dad was looking over his shoulder. "My gosh! Look at that!" he exclaimed. There in the dirt, lying completely exposed was a long, brown point. It must have been ten or twelve centimetres long. Lying there fully exposed, it was absolutely beautiful.

Slowly Mike reached down and picked it up. He held his breath as he turned it over and over in his hand and examined it. It was made of what looked to be more Knife River flint. The flakes of stone that had been expertly removed in its creation had left a pattern which his father had often described as parallel flaking. This meant the flakes on both sides of the blade had been removed directly opposite one another to create the keen cutting edge. The tip was needle-sharp. The base of the spear point tapered inwards slightly, and had no side notches; it had two small projections on the bottom corners.

Mike couldn't believe his eyes; his dad couldn't believe his either. Finally Mike let out a whoop which the wind carried over the coulee rim and into the river bottom. He had found it! The piece he had longed for and which he had secretly been searching for. Here it was! Mike wanted to run and jump and shout and throw things! And so did his dad! He too was extremely excited.

Laughing and talking loudly they headed back down the side of the coulee to the car. Mike kept the point in his hand and continually looked at it. As he walked down the steep hill, he stumbled and nearly fell because he couldn't tear his eyes away from the point in his hand.

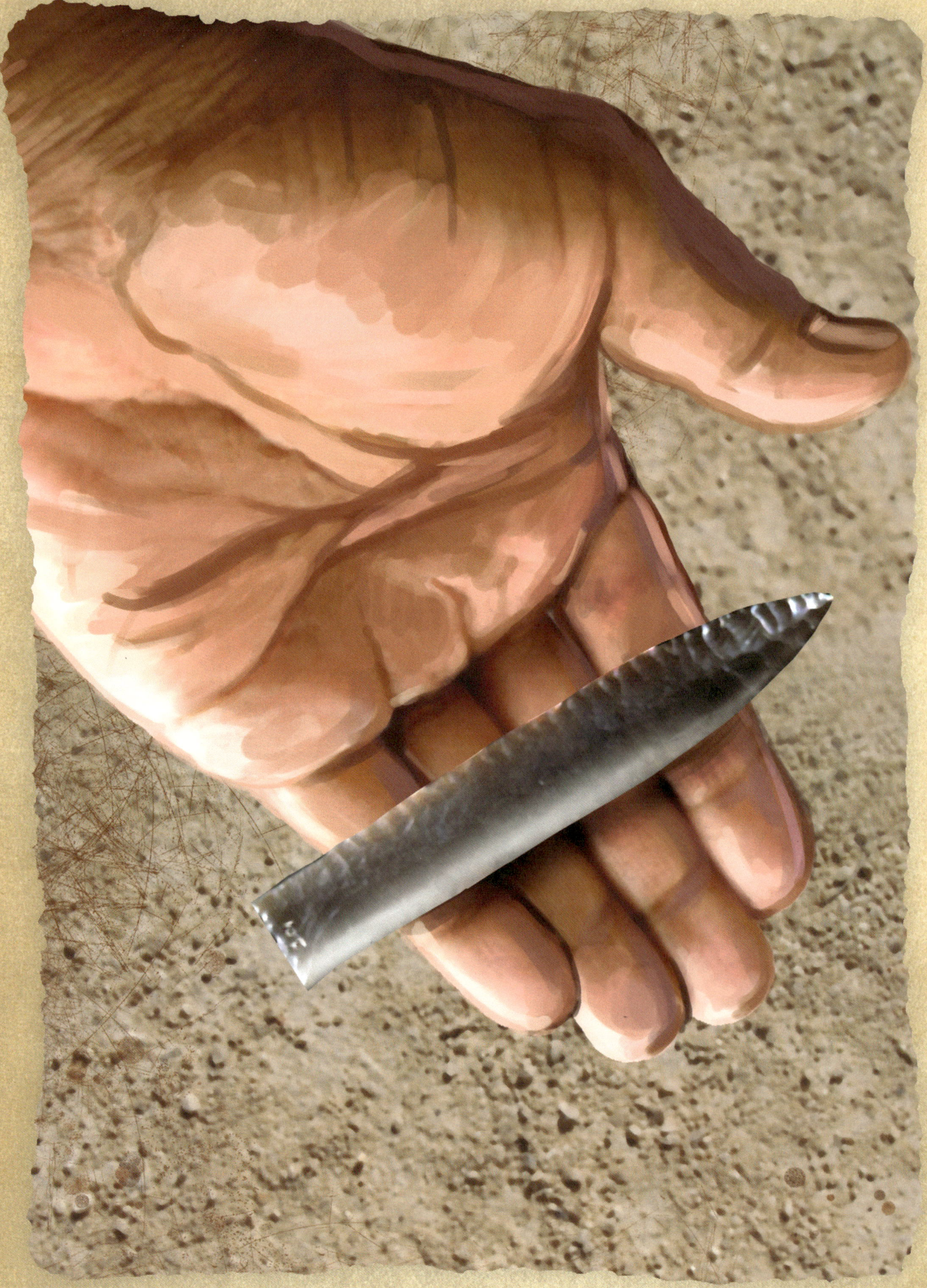

"Careful, son. Don't let that fall and break. Wow, is that ever something!" Mike laughed and said, "Don't worry! I'd rather break my leg than this spear point!" Nevertheless, he began looking more carefully at the ground in front of him.

As his father pulled the Volkswagen back onto the road and crossed the bridge, the west wind blew over the rock and bone fragments in the blow out, coursed over the coulee rim and charged down the hill through the grass. It gusted up again into the cottonwood trees, the branches of which clacked together in loud, rattling sounds. The dry leaves danced around the trunks of the trees and through the brush. As the gusting wind abated, a mournful sound carried across the land—but no one was there to hear.

That night, after Mike and his father had told their story of the day's adventures over and over to Mike's mother—adding more detail each time they told it—Mike finally realized that he was tired. And he was happy! He went to bed and as he lay there, he rolled over and looked at the beautiful point lying on his bedside table. In the darkness of his room, it showed up only as a dark object against the top of the table. He grinned to himself and reached out to touch it.

"Dad has never found such a fantastic point," he murmured. "Now I can show this off in our collection and everyone will know it was me who found it." As Mike drifted off to sleep, the last thing he heard was the wind moaning around the corner of the house.

CHAPTER 2

Daybreak was approaching. Naatosi, the sun, had already sent scouts out to lighten the sky on the horizon. The underbellies of the clouds showed the color of pink prairie flowers and the low, rolling hills, like rabbits huddled together, seemed to grow ever darker. In the darkness above and behind the camp, the screech of a hunting owl split the calm stillness of the morning.

As if this were a signal, Sopo, the west wind began to creep across the low-lying land. The grasses began to quiver and then lean, ever so slightly, and the leaves in the cottonwoods near the river began to whisper their early morning secrets. High above, the clouds seemed to quicken their pace and their pinkish tinge turned paler, and more yellow, like the breast feathers of a meadowlark. Somewhere near, the snorting of a horse carried clearly on the morning breeze.

Inside the tepee, Small Foot snuggled deeper under the buffalo robe. The cool morning air seemed determined to creep under the robe and wake him. His ears heard the early morning sounds—the owl, the horse and Sopo, the wind, but his mind didn't want to accept the end of the night. Then the sound of the wind grew louder and more insistent and Small Foot knew it was time to crawl out to meet the day.

Bull Shield, his father, had instructed Small Foot, that whenever he was away, Small Foot must rise early to greet the rising of the sun. By demonstrating his willingness to meet the sun, Naatosi would know that he was brave and honourable and would watch over him and his family during the day.

Quickly, Small Foot threw off the buffalo robe and headed out the entrance of the tepee. As he passed them in the dim morning light, he could see the humps on the ground surrounding the hearth that marked the sleeping robes of his mother, Willow that Bends in the Wind, and his sister, Falling Leaf. Glancing briefly to the rear of the tent, Small Foot reaffirmed that his father was not there. He thought briefly of his father's nervousness whenever he heard the screech of an owl before Naatosi peeked above the hills—but his father was not here to hear it. The entrance was covered with the tanned hide of a bison and as Small Foot pushed it aside, he stepped noiselessly outside the tepee. He knew that Naatosi would rise straight in front of him, as his father always oriented the door of the tepee to the rising sun.

The land was awakening. In the dusky light, Small Foot quickly checked the other four tepees that sheltered his father's brothers and their families. Smoke was already beginning to curl sleepily through the flaps at the top of the tepee nearest him.

Listening carefully, Small Foot tried to hear the secrets the cottonwood leaves were whispering. The guttural gurgling of the river splitting around stones near the shore seemed to grow fainter. "Shrrrieekk," the exuberant kill-cry of the owl came sliding in on the wind and Small Foot knew there was a dead mouse or gopher not far away. "Was it a bad omen?" he wondered.

Listening even more intently, Small Foot turned and faced the bluffs above the camp. The fresh wind blew the hair from his forehead and with the wind he heard the faint snickering and muffled clumps of the horse herd. His cousin, Calf, he knew, would be there with the horses, looking forward to coming back to camp to eat.

As he looked and listened, the first rays of the climbing sun touched the bluff-tops ever so gently, reminding Small Foot of his duties. Turning again to the rising sun, he stretched out his small arms and stared directly at the horizon where he knew Naatosi would shortly appear. In a small, but intently serious voice, Small Foot began singing his morning prayer:

> Naatosi, bringer of life and joy, Look down and see your son.
>
> As you climb your trail above, lighten my eyes to see the world.
>
> Help me to find food and happiness for my family today.
>
> Help me to recognize enemies by your light and protect my home.
>
> Naatosi, smile as you pass this way.

Staring unblinkingly at the morning sun as it showed itself above the horizon, Small Foot remained absolutely motionless until the orange morning orb had freed itself from the grasp of the hills and was started safely on its journey across the sky.

Blinking his eyes, Small Foot looked quickly around, pulled off his loincloth and ran with his limping gait quickly to the riverbank. Without pausing, he sprang high into the air and landed,

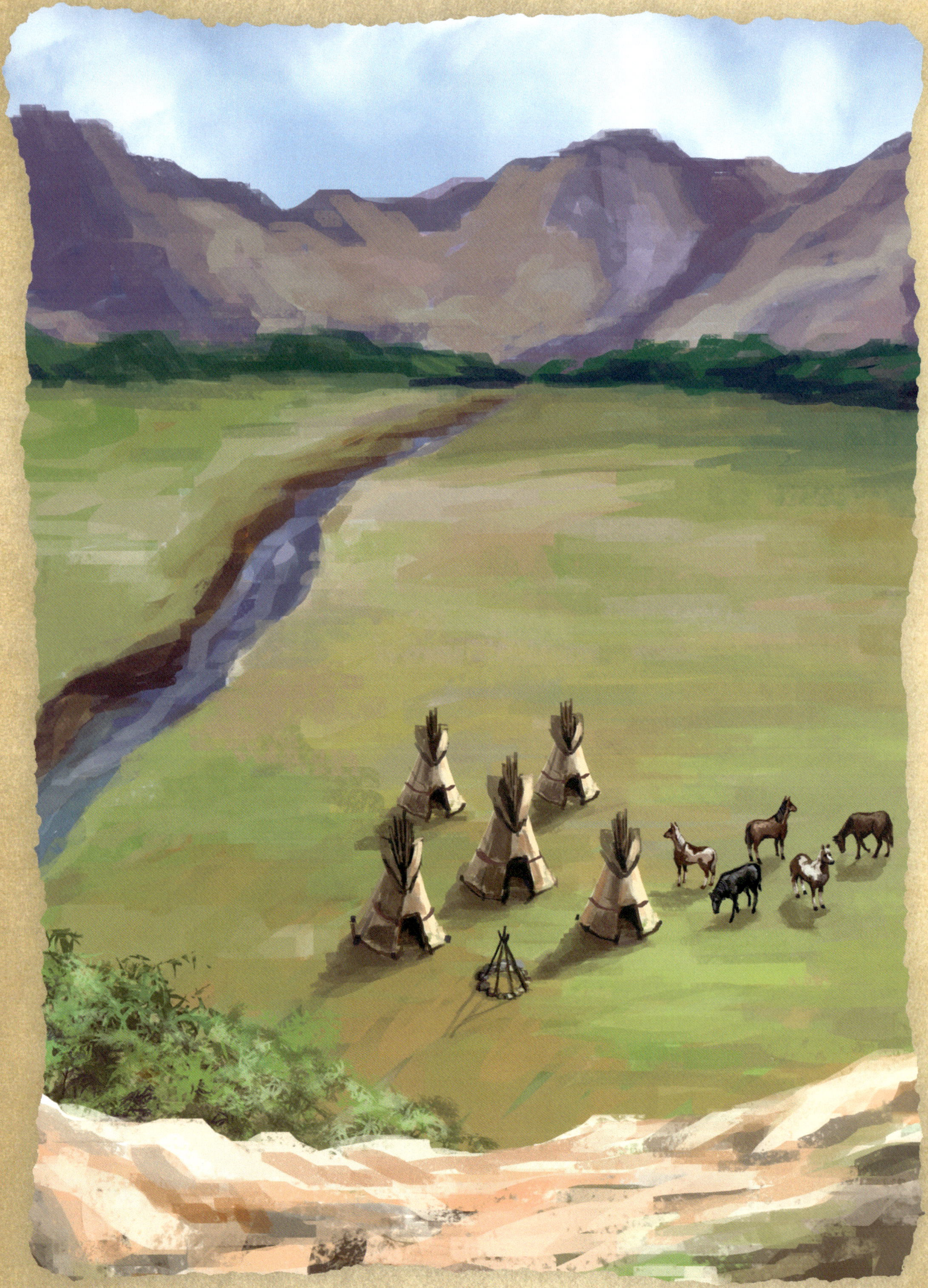

with a large splash, in the deep flow of the river. The cold water took his breath away, but chased away the sleep too. His head and upper body broke the surface of the water. "Ki yi yi yi ki!" his youthful voice laughingly carried his war-cry on the wind. Immediately several other splashes and cries were carried away on the wind as his cousins joined him in the water.

As smoke began to rise thinly from the top of his tepee, Small Foot splashed to the riverbank. Climbing out of the water, he quickly wiped the clusters of water drops from his body with his hands and jumped quickly up and down to dry himself. The breeze came to his aid and he was soon dry. After pulling his loincloth back around his hips, Small Foot walked quickly and silently to his lodge. Stooping into the entrance, Small Foot's eyes adjusted to the faint glow coming from the hearth; Falling Leaf was working near the fire and his mother, Willow, was rolling up the sleeping robes.

"Good morning, mother. Naatosi has given us another beautiful day!" "Yes, my son," replied Willow, "the day will be clear and warm. Eat some meat now to keep you strong. Today we will seek fresh meat and must work hard. Your father and uncles have gone to the killing place. We must take our places there soon."

Small Foot's heart seemed to leap within him. "Eie-yaii," he thought to himself, "today will be a great day. I must be ready." Briefly the ominous threat of the owl's kill-cry entered his head, but Small Foot had other things to think of and turned to his bundle of possessions lying near the side of the tent. Opening the parflech, the large satchel made from a stiff bison hide, Small Foot took out his medicine pouch. Inside were the objects which gave him strength and protected him.

The medicine pouch was small, a sack of soft deerskin which his mother had sewn for him. The top was closed with rawhide thongs which Small Foot now loosened. Reaching inside, the boy carefully extracted the contents. His fingers felt a small white perfectly smooth stone which Small Foot had found in a stream near the mountains. Shutting his eyes, Small Foot took the hard smoothness of the stone into his head and imagined its strength moving into his being. "May I be as strong and unchanging as this pebble," he muttered silently to himself.

He then pulled out the bone game sticks with the markings incised in them and laid them aside. Next, he grabbed a small bundle of sweet grass, tied together with a small, leather thong. Small Foot thought of putting some into the fire to taint the air with its sweet odour, but because time was short, he laid it aside as well. His hand disappeared again into the depths of the sack, feeling for the one, most coveted remaining item—the long, brown spear point which he knew was there. His fingers felt the cool sharpness of its edges as he pulled it out. The reflections of the lodge fire danced from its many surfaces as he looked at it. He smiled proudly to himself. "This will surely be strong medicine today! I will be brave and strong, powerful and deadly," he thought, "just like this spear point. Help my aim be true and my hunting success great!"

Looking fondly at the point, Small Foot's thoughts wandered back seven winters to the day his father gave him this powerful medicine.

CHAPTER 3

Bull Shield and his family had taken down their winter camp near the river. They had been there many moons during the cold and snowy days. They usually camped in the river bottoms under the large cottonwood trees as they provided shelter from the cold winds, were an easy source of wood for the fires and were near water. But when the warm wind began to blow and the snow melted, it was time to move the camp to the kill site near the mountains to participate in the spring bison hunt. Bull Shield was anxious to make the move as quickly as possible because early that morning he had heard the kill-cry of a hunting owl. Since the day when he was still a young brave and his father had been killed by horse thieves shortly after an owl had cried out early in the morning, he perceived this as a bad omen.

This had been Bull Shield's thirty-seventh winter. He was tall, with beautiful copper-colour skin and very dark hair which was parted in the middle. The scalp between the parts of his hair was painted a deep, almost blood-colour, red. He wore no braids today, but allowed his hair to hang over his shoulders and blow in the wind. He wore one simple, black-tipped eagle feather attached to his hair at the rear of his head, hanging downward. His upper torso was well-muscled and showed, both front and back, the scars of the sun dance when thongs of leather had broken free of chest and back muscles after several days of dancing and singing, while staring into the face of Naatosi. He wore a simple breech clout, hanging front and back and made from well-tanned deer hide. His legs were covered with long, porcupine decorated leggings which were tied to the belt around his waist and extended below his ankles. His feet were enclosed in beautifully quilled moccasins which Willow had worked on for several moons.

Bull Shield's wife, Willow Bends in the Wind, was carrying their newest child on a cradle board on her back. The daughter had been born in the middle of the coldest weather and had only just received her name—Falling Leaf. Her dark eyes were special as they turned toward each other when she looked out at the world around her. Small Foot had seen six winters and was now able, even though he limped when he walked, to help with small chores around the camps. He often fetched water from the river and carried it to the tepee in a leather bucket as well as tending to the horses as they grazed in the long grass or foraged for food during the day. He had also begun to develop his skills as a hunter and warrior, learning to track small animals and birds and to shoot straight with the bow and arrow. He was very proud to be given such responsibilities.

It wasn't difficult to move the camp as all of the family's possessions could easily be loaded on the travois which were pulled by the horses. The long lodge poles for the tepee made perfect supports for the travois and the family was soon on its way. As they made their way along the river bottom, Bull Shield rode his pony up onto the bluff above the river to look around. It was too early in the year to be too concerned about enemies coming to steal horses, but then, looking for the bison herds which were following the new grass on the prairies was always exciting.

On this day, Bull Shield had only just reached the top of the bluffs above the river when he saw an unusual sight. The spring winds had been blowing for many days and in some places it had blown the sandy soil away. He immediately noticed some very large bones exposed in the dirt. He rode his horse over to the bones and climbed down to look closer. The bones were very large and scattered about. Finding old bones was not unusual, but it gave Bull Shield an uneasy feeling nevertheless. The elders said that the "little people" often spread the bones about, and when one searched carefully, it was not unusual to find old arrow and spear points scattered among them.

As Bull Shield looked more closely, he saw an amazingly long, brown spear point. It lay just under the rib bones of the ancient animal. Bull Shield bent over and, very carefully, picked up the spear point and held it in his hand. The point was beautifully formed, obviously chipped from a larger piece of flint, and had been lying here for a very long time. One side of the rock point had turned nearly white. Reverently, Bull Shield placed the spear point into his medicine pouch which he carried around his neck. His thoughts immediately went back to the war-cry of the owl he had heard that morning and he wondered if this spear point might be medicine to ward off something evil.

For the rest of the day, Bull Shield and his family traveled slowly up the river valley, watching and carefully checking their progress by occasionally riding to the top of the valley and looking in all directions. Late in the afternoon, Bull Shield saw a telltale sign of dust in the air, coming from the next bend in the river. He immediately told his family to find cover in the deep brush growing along the river bank and to make sure the animals remained quiet. Sure enough, within a short time, seven warriors came riding silently down the trail. They were tribal enemies from across the mountains—Snakes! They were probably scouting the area for bison in order to report back to their tribe that the bison—linii—had arrived in this part of the country. Bull Shield and his family stayed hidden and silent as the warriors rode quietly past.

When the seven warriors finally disappeared around the next bend down the river, Bull Shield signalled his family to continue to head quietly in the other direction. He thought to himself, "The brown spear point must have been strong medicine. These are the enemies the owl warned me about this morning, and yet, with the spear point in my medicine pouch, they never even saw us." He knew it was important that they hurry to the rendezvous with other members of his tribe in order that he could report the whereabouts of these enemies.

For several more hours, Bull Shield and his family rode toward the killing place in the foothills of the mountains. Shortly after the long winter months ended, for as long as he could remember, Bull Shield's people had met at the killing place during the month of grass growing to kill the bison and prepare the meat to take care of them during the warm days and nights. They would meet in the same place again when the grass grew brown to kill linii before the onset of the cold moons. Most years there would be more than two hundred lodges camped at the bottom of the site and the people would work together for a successful hunt. As Bull Shield and his family came up out of the river bottom and headed toward the campsite, they could see that already many lodges had been erected and a large encampment was taking shape.

Willow and Bull Shield immediately selected a site for their tepee in the circle of their closest family and friends. All of the tepees were erected with their entrances facing the rising sun and the campsite therefore was shaped like the breast bone of a prairie chicken—curved on the sides and open at one end. While Willow and Small Foot began unloading the travois and preparing the tepee to be set up, Bull Shield hurried to the tent of the family leader and elder and asked to speak to him. They entered his tepee and sat near the small fire that had been set in the middle of the tent. After greetings and polite conversation about the cold days and nights, Bull Shield said, "Today I saw seven Snake warriors riding through the river bottom. They were astride good horses, and while they were not painted for war, their weapons were ready for use. They are likely the scouts for a tribe of Snakes who wait in the passes of the mountains to come to the flat lands to hunt linii. What should we do?" The old man was silent for what seemed like a long time, and then said, "The Snake children need to eat too; they are unfortunate that the linii do not find homes on the other side of the mountains. Therefore, as long as they leave us and our horses alone, we will leave them alone."

Bull Shield left the tent and returned to his family to find that they were nearly finished with the setting up of camp. He was proud of Willow and Small Foot, as they seemed able to function well without him.

Early the next morning, Small Foot went out to the large horse herd, found Bull Shield's ponies and took them, two at a time, down to the river for water. It was one of the many chores which his father entrusted to him. After he had watered six horses and was returning to fetch the last two, he heard strange whisperings coming from the brush surrounding the grazing area. He thought at first it was his cousins playing a trick on him to scare him, so he decided to sneak up on them and scare them instead. After securing the two horses to a tree, he crept silently through the brush. He suddenly realized the whispering was not coming from his friends at all, but was in fact the musing of strange looking warriors studying the horse herd. Small Foot immediately stopped crawling, lay very still and observed the men. It was obvious that they were preparing to run off some of the horse herd. Small Foot crawled slowly backwards, climbed on his father's brown and white pony and turned it back to camp. He kept the horse under control and quiet, walking slowly by the river until he had gone around the bend. Then, he kicked the horse's flanks and ran it as fast as he could back to the camp.

As he pulled the pony to a skidding stop in front of the family tent, Bull Shield came out of the entrance to meet him. "Father, father! There are enemies near the horse herd! They are preparing to steal horses!" Bull Shield immediately called aloud in the camp, "Warriors! Prepare yourselves and accompany me to the horses. The Snakes are stealing them! Come quickly!"

Picking up his bow, arrows and a spear, Bull Shield jumped on the pony Small Foot had been riding and rushed in the direction of the herd. Right behind him came several warriors, some running on foot and others on horses that had been tethered near the camp circle. As they neared the grazing horses, they saw Snake warriors riding off in the opposite direction with about twenty head of horses. With war whoops, the men of the camp followed as fast as horses could carry them. The departing Snakes saw them coming, forgot about the horses they were herding and headed out toward the river as fast as they could go. Two of the warriors were on foot and had not had time to mount horses. They were easily overrun and Bull Shield and his men quickly surrounded them.

Bull Shield rode forward and hit the taller of the two across the face with his bow. He shouted and signed with his hands, "Why are you here? We would share the linii with you, as we understand you have family at home who must eat. But to steal our horses in our land? This cannot go unpunished." He nodded his head at the others and said, "Let them run." The warriors moved out of the way and the Snakes turned and began to run away. Bull Shield cocked his arm and quickly threw his spear. It pinioned the taller Snake in the back and he fell awkwardly to the ground and died. The others whooped and yelled as the other Snake warrior ran for the river, reached the high bank, and then jumped into the water. They shouted and taunted him as he was swept downstream away from them. Bull Shield dismounted, strode over to the fallen warrior, grabbed his hair and swiftly cut it from his head. He brandished the scalp in the air and let out his loudest war whoop. In addition to sending a message to the remaining Snake warriors, this would be strong medicine for the hunt that was to come.

Returning to camp with the rest of his friends, Bull Shield called his son, Small Foot, to the campfire and in a large voice, so all could hear, proclaimed, "This is my son, Small Foot. Even though he has few winters, this morning he has acted bravely and cleverly for the good of all of us. He warned us of the attack of thieves on our most prized possession, our horses. In recognition of his bravery, I bestow on him the following strong medicine." He reached into his medicine pouch and withdrew the long, brown spear point which he had picked up the previous day. "This spear point, left for us by the little people, I now give to you my son in recognition of your bravery and cleverness. From this point forward, you will be recognized as a brave of our family and will be honoured as such. You will learn the ways of the hunter and warrior and will become a respected and powerful member of our tribe! We are all proud of you!"

Small Foot was proud and excited. He took the spear point from his father and placed it into his medicine pouch, vowing that he would always carry it as a reminder of this day.

CHAPTER 4

Small Foot remembered the time with pleasure and pride, but knew it was time to begin working. Following a quick meal of dried bison, Small Foot helped his mother and sister take down the tepee and wrap all other possessions in bison robes. These they tied to the travois and attached the lodge poles to three of the horses. The others and their families were doing the same and within a short time they were all ready for the move to the killing site. The small group headed up out of the river bottom and began the journey across the prairie. Small Foot and two cousins rode ahead to scout out the trail and to make sure there was no sign of trouble on their route. The journey lasted most of the day, but as evening approached, they spotted the smoke from the fires of those already camped below the ridges. Small Foot rode quickly ahead and saw his father, Bull Shield, standing and waiting anxiously for their arrival. He dismounted quickly in front of his father and greeted him. "We are well, father. Mother and Falling Leaf are only a short time behind and will be here soon. We have seen no enemy and no linii. Nevertheless, we are excited to see you and look forward to the hunt." Of course, Small Foot was confident that he, while having lived only ten and three winters, would this year have a significant role in the bison hunt and kill. He could hardly wait!

Shortly thereafter, the small family group arrived and there was much gaiety and joy as they set up their camps in the traditional manner. Bull Shield was proud of the efficiency of his family. They had learned well. The tepee was erected near the center of the camp as befitted the honours Bull Shield had as an elder within the tribe. He was one of the more prominent warriors and spent much of his time talking and planning with the other leaders.

Several days passed by and still no large bison herds were spotted. There were isolated small groups of bison on the prairie, but the large bison herds were nowhere to be found. Bull Shield and the others were not concerned. It was often like this. He knew that as the new grass grew taller and riper, the bison herds would not be far behind. The winds blowing out of the mountains were still cool and refreshing and the river water at night often had a thin coat of ice on it. However, because the grass was nutritious and plentiful, the horses were becoming strong and fat after the winter. There was plenty of work to do. In addition to making arrows and spears, the stone workers were kept busy making points and tools. Small Foot and his friends made several trips to the mountain pass to find the special stones from which to make tools. It was an important role in the life of his people, and Small Foot was proud to have the ability required to recognize and find the stones. He found that when the sun was shining high in the sky, he could sit on the edge of a mountain stream and eventually pick out the rocks under the fast flowing water. His friends were often amazed at his talent and the stone workers of the tribe nodded knowingly to each other, thinking that here was a young brave who would eventually learn their craft.

Bull Shield and the others went out every day to search for the indicators of the approaching bison herds. They went up on the rocks in the high places and sat for hours watching the horizon in the direction of the rising sun, hoping for the telltale clouds of dust which would announce their arrival. Later in the day, they wandered from rock pile to rock pile in the drive lines, making sure they were high enough to hide a hunter and that they were perfectly placed. The drive lines were located above the kill site and stretched back considerable distances from the cliffs. The rock piles were placed in lines the width of the small mountain streams apart so that they would be able to keep the running and nervous bison moving in the correct direction. The area between the lines was wider where it began in the high grass; as the lines drew nearer to the cliff ahead, the area grew ever narrower. The effect was similar to water flowing in the rivers—where the banks were far apart, the river was wide and slow moving. Where the banks came close together, the river became narrow and deep and the current was much faster. The same principle worked with the running bison; they were between the drive lines before they knew it and it was all slow and easy, but as they continued to graze in the direction of the cliffs, the area became more confining and forced the bison to bunch up and become crowded and nervous. Eventually, the people hiding behind the piles of stone would begin to shout and wave bison robes at the animals. They would become agitated and begin running. It was then only a matter of keeping them running in the appropriate direction—and that direction led eventually to the cliffs and the kill site.

As the weather warmed, the grasses grew green as the new grass replaced the old. And finally, one afternoon, Bull Shield came back to camp with exciting news—large bison herds had been spotted. Now it was just a matter of days before bison would wander up into the hills behind the kill site and the people could begin to position them for the eventual hunt.

Small Foot was excited because this year he had been selected to take a position behind one of the rock piles in the drive line. While he wouldn't be allowed too close to the edge of the cliff—that was reserved for the older and more experienced—nevertheless he would participate! He had already climbed the hills and hiked to his pile many times so that he would know exactly where he was to go and what he was to do. Many of his friends had the same opportunity and were as excited as he.

Five of the older boys had been selected to be the coyotes. They would wear the hides of coyotes which had been stretched and sewn for this purpose. Their responsibility would be to crawl around the bison as they grazed, keeping them nervous and bunched up enough to herd them in the right direction. They would eventually keep the animals moving in a group toward the cliffs. The boys who were in front of the moving herd were the fastest runners because they would eventually have to run to get out of the way of the stampeding herd. It was a dangerous and respected responsibility—only last year, Beaver Tail had been stomped into the ground and killed when he didn't get out of the way fast enough. Nevertheless, Small Foot hoped that one day he too would be able to assume this honourable opportunity as a coyote. But it wouldn't happen this year.

Small Foot spent considerable time observing and exploring the area around their camp. When he didn't understand something, he would ask Bull Shield to explain it to him. The actual killing site was at the bottom of the cliffs which stretched for a considerable distance along the bluffs at the end of the drive lines. While the cliffs were fairly high, nevertheless, the animals were not generally killed by the fall. They would break bones—legs, necks and backs, but they would still be alive. The oldest and most experienced hunters would be placed at the bottom of kill site where they would dispatch the animals as they landed on the ground beneath the cliffs. They would kill them with arrows and would have several quivers full of arrows at their disposal. Depending on the number of animals that eventually fell over the cliffs, they could potentially shoot hundreds of arrows into the struggling mass. Once this killing had been accomplished, the real work began. Willow that Bends in the Wind and the other women from the camp would move into the pile of dead animals, and with the help of the men, begin the excruciating work of skinning the animals and butchering their carcasses.

Not one bit of the bison would be wasted. In addition to the meat, the hides, horns, hooves, testicles, tails and even the bones were saved. It took several days for the butchering process to be completed. The warm sun would make many days unbearable as the stench of the rotting carcasses often became overpowering. Small Foot realized that it was for good reason that the kill sites were most often situated on bluffs or hills on the side opposite from where the sun rose.

The winds would work together with the people to ensure that the bison couldn't smell the kill site and turn away.

Small Foot and his family knew it was imperative to the well-being of the people that enough meat was harvested during this hunt to keep everyone well supplied for several moons. One of the harder jobs was to cut the meat into strips, dry it in the sun by laying it in the hot sun on a rock, and then pounding it into almost a powder which was mixed with grease and berries to preserve it. The women of the people worked very hard to accomplish this task. In addition, clothing, weapons, sleeping robes and tepee skins had to be manufactured from the hides of the animals. Small Foot had watched his mother work long, hard days to prepare the hides for their use. Truly, the bison hunts were the most important single event in the lives of the people of the plains.

CHAPTER 5

The morning came early on the day of the hunt. Small Foot threw off his robes and was out of the tent before anyone else was stirring. He was tremendously excited because the elders had indicated that today was the day. As he looked to the far horizon, he could see an indistinct lightening of the sky. Naatosi would make his appearance soon. Small Foot reached to his medicine pouch and felt the spear point. "Hopefully this will bring me great luck today. I wish to become a great hunter and warrior like my father. His medicine has always been very powerful and the point will work for me," he thought. At that moment, he heard the shrill Kriieeek of the owl. "He too would make a significant kill this morning," mused Small Foot, and then remembered that his father was not happy to hear this sound. But, on such an exciting morning, he forgot about it.

At the same time, Bull Shield, lying under his sleeping robe, heard the kill-cry too. He tried not to think of it as a bad omen and realized that the owl too must make kills in order to live. He climbed out from under his bison robe and moved to the coals in the center of the tepee. He reached into his medicine pouch and pulled out some dried sweet grass stalks and dropped them into the fire. The coals immediately burned the dried grass and white smoke rose from the fire. With the pungent aroma and the visible smoke, Bull Shield offered a silent prayer to the heavens, asking for a successful and safe hunt. He turned and climbed out of the tepee entrance and was not surprised to see Small Foot awaiting him. "Good morning, son. This will be an important day for you. Run like the wind and make me proud of you."

Small Foot smiled and turned to find his friends who also must make the long climb to the far end of the drive lanes. They gathered in the center of the camp and waited for the final instructions from the hunter in charge. After they had all gathered, Black Plume moved out among them and called for their attention. "Hear me! Today is an important day for you and your people. You must hurry to your assigned locations behind the rock piles high in the hills. There you must wait quietly for the bison to awake and begin grazing. As they move closer to your locations, you must remain as still as the mountain rocks until they have moved past you. As the linii move further into our trap, you will have to move quickly from one pile of rock to the next. You can allow the animals to see you as you move in the lines, but do not spook them and cause them to run. The linii have bad eyes and will not know what they are seeing, but they will be nervous. That is good because when it is time for them to run, they will charge in the direction we want them to. Remember, do not scare the linii until you hear my whistle. I will blow through the leg of the prairie chicken and you will know that it is time for the stampede. You will know the time has come to make noise when the hunters wearing coyote hides begin to move the herd down the final drive lane. By that time the herd should be large—it will be up to the coyotes to ensure that many linii are in the stampeding herd. Each of you has his duty; do it well and the people will not starve."

With that, Black Plume dismissed the young boys and they headed up onto the prairie at the top of the cliffs. The sun was still sleeping below the distant horizon and they had to step carefully in order to not make noise and to be safe. Small Foot with his limp was careful to place his moccasins exactly in the same places as the boy in front of him. He did not want to be the one to disturb the bison and be disgraced.

Once on top of the bluffs, the boys slowed down and began to walk silently and cautiously to their positions. The practices they had carried out during the many days previous were valuable. They were able to find their way with little trouble, even though they could not see well. Here and there in the darkness they were able to see the dark outlines of animals lying in the grass sleeping. They moved around these animals as carefully and quietly as possible. Occasionally they could hear the snorting and snuffling of bison that were already awake and beginning to feed. These they were most careful to avoid as they were alert.

The wind was blowing softly from the direction of the mountains and the bison could not smell the boys nor hear them well. Slowly and quietly, the young hunters passed the animals and moved to the other side of them. Small Foot was happy to eventually arrive at his pile of stones. He immediately took the robe which he wore over his shoulders and placed it on the ground behind the stones. He then lay down and began the wait. As his eyes became more and more adjusted to the darkness, he noticed that there were far more bison in the vicinity than he had ever seen. There were large bulls wandering about and cows and calves still lying on the ground sleeping. Small Foot could feel the excitement building in his stomach and he could hardly wait for the signal from Black Plume that the hunt should begin. However, he knew that they would have to wait for Naatosi to climb much higher into the sky.

It seemed like forever before the sky began to lighten and shadows on the ground slowly disappeared. As the first rays of light began to move across the grasslands, Small Foot realized that the day was truly beginning. He knew that by now, Bull Shield and the other chosen hunters would have moved into position below the cliffs and would be preparing their arrows for the coming kill. Small Foot noticed that the individual stalks of grass around him began to appear and realized that it was definitely becoming easier to see. He could now make out the piles of rocks across the drive lane from him and those that wended their way down toward the cliffs. He knew that all rock piles did not have hunters behind them, but that as the piles came closer to the cliffs, more hunters were squatted there waiting.

The anticipation made him nervous. The female and young bison too were beginning to awaken and move about. He could hear the noises of their waking and the stomping of the ground as they got to their feet. Looking around the rocks, he could now see that most of the animals in his vicinity were up and grazing in the grass. He could even begin to see the movement of their purple tongues as they grasped the grass and pulled it into their mouths. The chomping of the white teeth as they bit through the grass and swallowed became discernable to his ears. Even the calves were beginning to feed beside their mothers, nudging their sides with their heads, looking for warm milk.

The wind was beginning to blow even stronger and the sounds of the bison were becoming more and more distinct. Small Foot could even hear the slurping of the calves as they fed. The wind was good as it made it much more difficult for the bison to hear any sounds that might have been inadvertently made by the hunters. The day was going to be perfect!

Finally, Naatosi appeared on the horizon. His circular head began to appear just above the flatlands in colors of gold, yellow and pink. It was possible to actually see the movement of the sun as he climbed higher into the sky. Small Foot could hardly contain his excitement! He looked around the pile of stones in front of him and saw the hunters masquerading as coyotes begin to crawl out into the drive lane. They came on very slowly, crawling on all fours and often stopping to sniff the air. Small Foot noticed one old bull, not far from him, lift his shaggy head and stare in the direction of the coyotes. His tail swished and his eyes rolled, but he did not move. He would keep a close watch on the animals, but for the time being, there was very little threat. His head went back down to the luscious grass at his feet.

The coyote hunters split up and began to crawl around the sides of the large bunches of bison feeding in the drive lane. Two remained at the far end of the bison to keep them from moving in that direction while the others began to move around the outer edges of the feeding groups. The bison acknowledged their presence by beginning to slowly move closer to the center of the drive lane—and to each other. Small Foot could see that the separate groups of feeding bison would slowly move into one larger group of animals. He knew that this was necessary in order for the drive to be successful and marvelled at the skills demonstrated by the young hunters. They continued to crawl slowly around the outer edges of the feeding bison and very casually moved the animals together.

Sopo, the west wind, was now blowing with force. The bison continued to feed on the grass, but slowly turned their bodies so their backs and hind legs were facing the wind. This resulted in the herd movement beginning to meander in the direction of the killing cliffs. As yet, the movement was slow and subtle, and Small Foot and his friends behind the rock piles had to exert significant patience. It was still not the time for the herd to move swiftly; in fact, if it continued slowly in the direction it was moving, everything would be perfect.

By now a couple of the coyote hunters had moved in front of the larger bunch of bison and were effectively thwarting any other bison to join the herd from in front. Those bison in the front of the intended herd saw the coyotes ahead of them and continued to graze away from the coyotes. Small Foot knew that this was the intention of the experienced hunters as the herd could not be too large when it finally stampeded. There were a number of reasons why this was necessary, all learned through generations of hunting experience. Bull Shield and the other hunters had told the younger boys that too many bison created a herd that could not be controlled. It would tend to go where it wanted to go and not in the direction the hunters intended. Also, too many animals plunging off the cliffs created a problem for the hunters below—they could not kill all of the wounded animals effectively and many would eventually be wasted. Nevertheless, it was important to have a reasonably large number of bison in the herd, as they would run as a group and follow the leaders. They would not be able to see ahead of the animals in front of them and the group would move blindly over the cliffs.

Small Foot noticed that the herd of bison was directly in front of his rock pile. There were cows, calves and monstrous bulls in the group. They were now moving slowly in the direction of the cliffs and the timing seemed appropriate to Small Foot. He thought that at any moment Black Plume would blow the chicken bone whistle and the most important part of the hunt would begin.

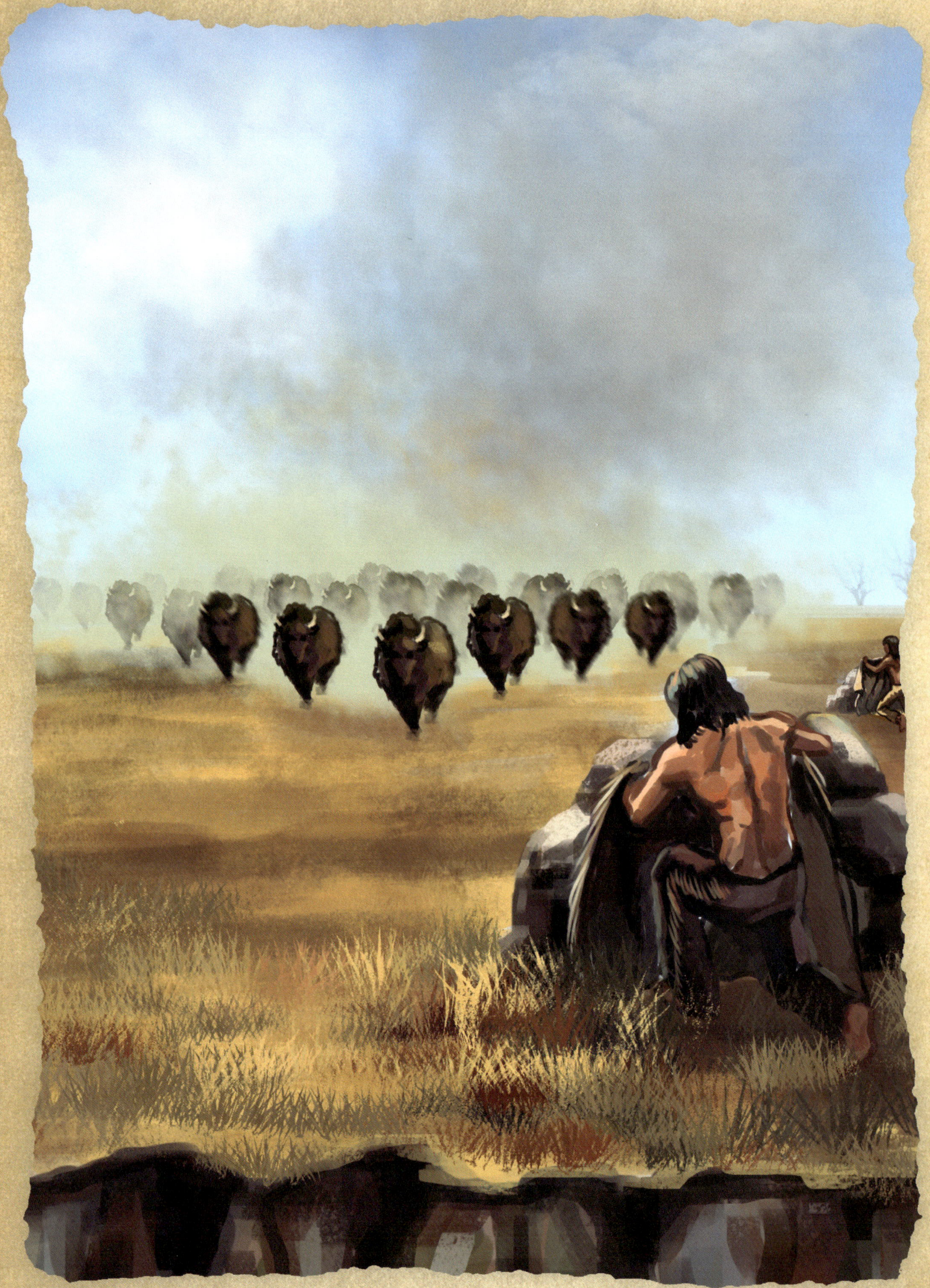

And then it happened! Screeeeeeeeeeeeeeeeet! The sound of the whistle came flying downwind—it was time! Small Foot, in unison with the other young hunters behind the stone piles, jumped up, grabbing his robe and waving it in the wind, all the while screaming at the top of his lungs. The noise and confusion was startling! The bison heads came up—their small eyes rolling in the sockets looking for the source of the noise. Tails went straight up in the air and as a group they began to run, shying away from the noise and the flapping bison hides. Their feet seemed hardly to touch the ground and their braying and snorting added to the overall confusion.

Small Foot could see that the large herd of bison was already moving into rapid flight. The cows with their calves had moved into the center of the stampeding herd and were running as hard as they could. The bulls had moved to the outside of the herd and were snorting and roaring. Watching down the drive lane, Small Foot could see that the hunters behind the rock piles were timing their appearance with the movement of the herd. As it thundered by their locations, the hunters would jump to their feet and add their noise and movement to the chaotic flight of the herd. The coyote hunters in front of the herd had now jumped to their feet and were running as fast as they could to get out of the way of the charging bison. Their purpose had been served and it was now every man for himself trying to run to safety away from the slashing danger of the flying hooves.

Small Foot and the other younger hunters began to run and scream and yell behind the herd. The bison were running so fast that they could not catch them, but the young hunters would not be denied the end of the hunt. Their presence also ensured that the stampeding animals would not turn back into the wind and run away. Instead, the animals were trying to put as much distance as possible between themselves and the howling, screaming noise behind their backs. Here and there an individual bison would dodge out between the rock piles, but most were caught up in the herd mentality of the stampeding animals and moved quickly toward their ultimate doom. Small Foot noticed a calf, bawling for its mother, running away in obvious terror through the grass. And here and there an animal lay on the ground after having tripped in its flight and not being able to regain its feet.

The scene was truly spectacular! Here was a large herd of bison running at full-tilt before the wind, trying to escape the people who had brought such terror and confusion to the day. The animals had created a large dust cloud, even though they were running through grass; visibility had become difficult. The noise created by the bellowing and roaring of the bison, combined with the thunderous sounds of hooves hitting the ground, had now drowned out the sounds and shouts of the hunters. The animals were moving so quickly and closely bunched together that there was no longer any escape. The animals in front were being pressed by those behind and those behind were blinded by the ones in front. The surging backs of the bison were all that could be seen in the large clouds of billowing dust and all too that the bison themselves could see. Those at the head of the herd could see the prairies in the distance, but their eyes under these circumstances were not keen enough to recognize that there was a drop off in front of them. In fact, they ran as if they had a wide-open prairie in front of them and like they knew they would eventually be able to outrun the trouble behind them.

As Small Foot and the others watched, the lead bison came to the edge of the cliff, and although they tried to stop and turn, the pressure of those behind forced them over the cliff—and those following came closely behind. In a very short time, the large herd of bison that had been driven through the drive lanes to the killing site at the cliffs was gone. They had all dropped to their deaths.

At the bottom of the cliffs, Bull Shield and many other hunters were waiting. They had their weapons ready—spears and bows and arrows. As the ground began to shake and the noises of the hunt rode in to them on the wind, the warriors knew too it was time. Suddenly, the beasts were very close; the noise had become deafening and clouds of dust raised by the hooves of the animals swirled around them. And then, the first line of bison was at the edge of the cliff. Their eyes were rolling in their heads and their mouths were wide open, gasping for air and bellowing all at the same time. Bull Shield and the other hunters knew what to expect; they had done this many times before. They stood back from the cliffs—far enough that none of the animals could fall on them—but close enough that they could immediately begin to kill the wounded animals.

As the lead bison hurtled through the air, the hunters drew back their bows and began shooting into the mass of bodies. The thunderous concussions of these large animals hitting the ground were unnerving, but the hunters knew that killing all of them was imperative. On this day, the hunt went off precisely as planned. No animals escaped the headlong rush to the cliffs and no animals were able to turn away. They landed hard at the foot of the cliffs and were immediately met with a shower of arrows. Broken legs and backs caused the animals to wail in pain and fright, and their squeals and clamour added to the confusion. The hunters continued to shoot into the mass of bodies as they continued to land at their feet after falling from the top of the cliff.

Bull Shield realized that the number of bison was large—usually the pile of broken bodies only reached halfway back up the cliff face. But this time, they seemed to keep coming. The last animals to fall over the top landed on bodies stacked high in the air. Several of the smaller calves and cows landed into the pile and were unhurt. These animals quickly stumbled and jumped their way to freedom and ran off down the steep hill. Some had arrows sticking out of their hides where the hunters had shot them, but in many cases they were not seriously injured and were able to make their getaway.

As the herd finished falling off the cliff, the hunters began moving around the large pile of bodies in order to direct their murderous fire into all of the animals. Bull Shield ran around to the side of the bodies nearest the bottom of the cliffs and continued shooting arrows into the mass. He like many of the other hunters had already shot away most of the hunting arrows and was now using even the arrows intended for shooting small game and birds. The stone points on these arrows were very small, but that was all that was available and they had to be used.

Meanwhile, Small Foot, at the top of the cliffs, noticed another small herd of bison running furiously in the direction of the drop off. He, together with several other young hunters, tried desperately to turn these animals aside by waving robes and screaming. However, because of the limited visibility and the chaos, these animals, two bulls, a cow and two calves, headed directly for the cliff edge and followed the herd that had passed there moments earlier. They too ran straight over the edge.

At the bottom of the cliff, Bull Shield had exhausted his supply of arrows, including his bird arrows, and now gripped the strong wooden handle of his spear. He began to climb onto the pile of dead and dying animals to stab any bison still moving. Just as he had stuck his spear point into the throat of an enormous bull, he heard the sound of other animals above him. Without looking up, he jumped directly backwards off the pile of animals, trying to get as close to the cliff face as possible. At that moment, a large bull landed on his head and knocked him down onto the pile. Another bison landed on top of him and he was immediately crushed under the tremendous weight of the five animals which had come over the cliff. When the dust settled and the sounds dissipated, the other hunters rushed to find Bull Shield in the pile of broken bodies.

Pulling him by his feet from the mangled animals, his friends realized that he was no longer

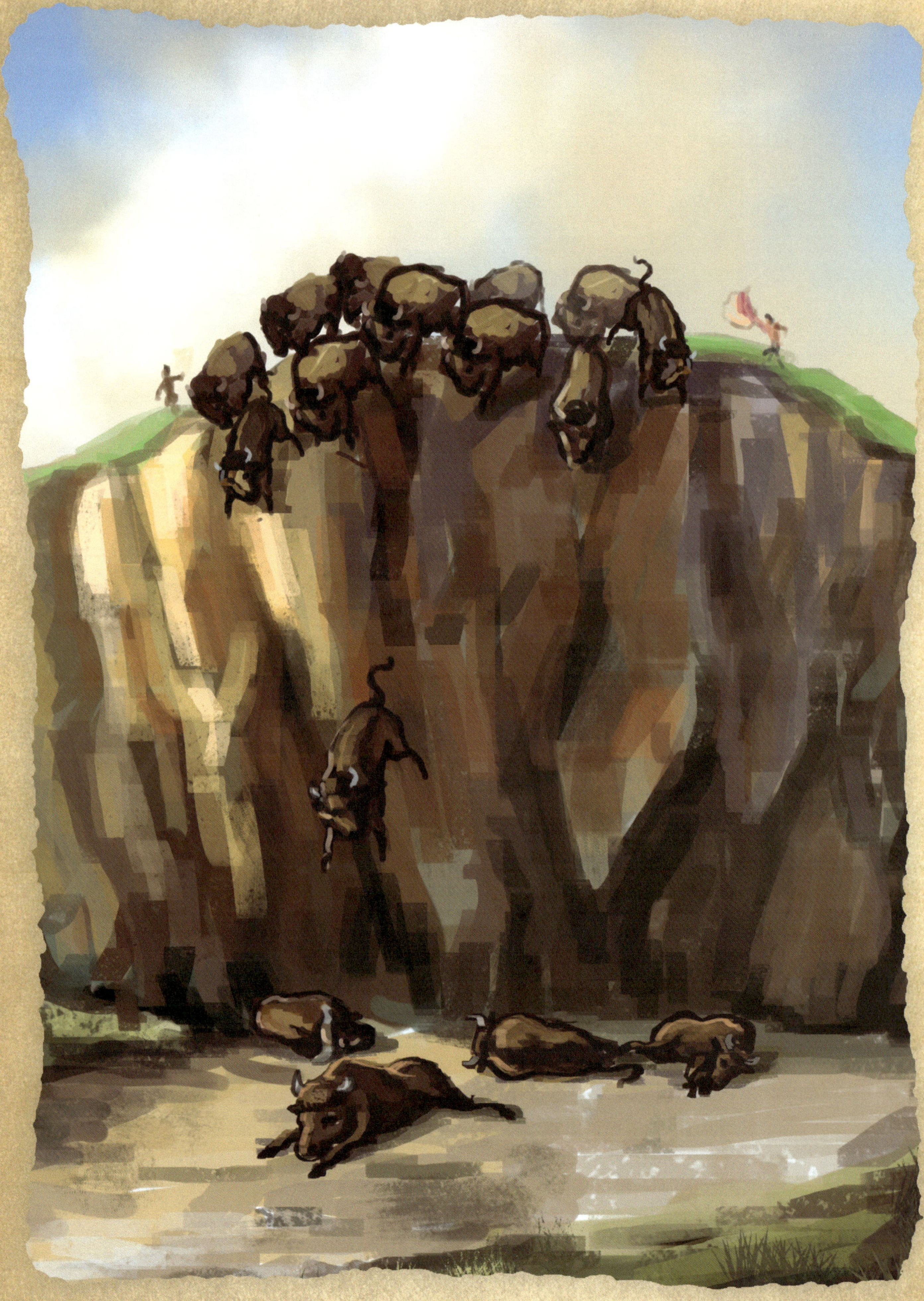

alive. His head had been smashed by the weight of the falling animals, with blood and other liquids seeping out of his skull. They immediately began singing a death song and the women and children who were waiting further below the kill site knew that someone had died. Small Foot heard the singing and keening of the hunters below and it immediately reminded him of the kill-cry of the owl which he and Bull Shield had heard early this morning. His heart began to beat faster and he knew he had to quickly make his way to the bottom of the cliffs.

Small Foot ran all the way back to the area where the cliffs were less steep and stumbled down the hill to the ground below the bluff. Ahead of him he could see the great pile of dead bison and large numbers of the people standing and climbing around the pile. As he came running to the side of the pile nearest the cliffs, he could see his mother, Willow Bends in the Wind, kneeling and crying near the body of a warrior. Small Foot immediately recognized the moccasins and leggings and knew that his father lay there. Kneeling quickly by his mother's side, Small Foot saw that his father's eyes were open, but that they had glazed over, much like the eyes of the bison in the killing pile. He noticed too that his father had blood running out of his ears and mouth. A terrible sense of dread permeated his heart and mind and he knew that his father was dead. His mother began keening and moaning and had already grabbed a stone knife and gashed her arms and forehead. Her blood flowed freely and mixed with the blood of Bull Shield.

Several hours after the incident, Bull Shield's body had been carried back to their tepee and the butchering of the dead animals had begun. Small Foot, his sisters and mother did not participate in the butchering, but remained in the camp with the body of Bull Shield. They all mourned his death and cried and sang death songs for several hours. The elders had approached her outside her tepee and told her that they would forever refer to this kill site as the place where "His head was smashed in", in honour of Bull Shield.

Early the next morning, as the sun rose over the far horizon, Small Foot and Willow began packing up their camp. They wrapped Bull Shield in a large bison robe and lay him on a travois. Once they had everything organized, they began the trek back to Bull Shield's favourite campsite in the river bottoms. The other people assured them that they would meet up with them in several days and that they would bring the dried bison meat that they would need for the coming summer season.

Small Foot was now the eldest male member of his family and felt the responsibilities immediately. His mother already deferred to him the obligation of leading the family with their horses and possessions to the river bottom. Small Foot rode his father's favourite war pony and moved out in front of the family to ensure safe passage. He felt extremely sad and concerned and believed that his father had died because his medicine had somehow failed him. He recalled his father's concern about the kill-cry of the owl that fateful morning and further, that his father had presented him with his spear point—a significant part of his personal medicine.

Several hours later, after reaching the campsite, Small Foot and his mother set up the tepee and organized a camp. They then placed Bull Shield's body inside and removed his hunting clothing. Willow prepared Bull Shield's ceremonial clothing, and once the blood and dirt had been cleaned from his body, dressed Bull Shield in his finery. The moccasins, leggings and war shirt were all decorated with beautifully dyed porcupine quills. The items were all made from carefully tanned deer skin and were soft and nearly white. Willow combed out Bull Shield's hair and carefully made two braids, which she placed over his shoulders. The braids' ends she covered with deer hide strips. In his hair she placed his two eagle feathers which signified his war and bravery exploits and around his neck she placed his medicine pouch and his necklace of bear claws and bone beads. When all was finished, she and her family wept over the body. They lifted Bull Shield onto a bison robe and carried and dragged him out to the travois. They placed him on the lodge poles and attached them to the horse. Moving slowly, Small Foot, accompanied by his mother and sisters led the horse slowly up onto the high bluffs overlooking the slowly flowing river.

Once they reached the top of the bluff, they spread another robe on the ground and together lifted and carried Bull Shield onto the robe. They all took a few moments to say their private goodbyes to Bull Shield and then wrapped him tightly in the robe. Leaving him high on the bluff was difficult, but to people who were used to violent death and loss, the process was understandable and natural.

Small Foot was unable to sleep well that night, and while the sky was still black, he wriggled out of his sleeping robe and crawled out of the tepee. Looking up to the bluff where his father lay, Small Foot made his decision. He walked quickly and silently back up the steep hill to the top of the bluff. There he contemplated the bundle that contained his father, and then quickly stooped and opened the robe. Reaching into the pouch around his own neck, he pulled out the spear point his father had given him, and placed it on his father's chest next to the medicine bundle. He sat there very still and remained there until Naatosi began his trail across the sky. When the rays of the sun reached him high on the bluff, he murmured, "Father...I give you your powerful medicine back as you will need it in the next life. Carry it with pride and love, knowing that I, Small Foot, love you and will always think of you as I experience my own adventures in this life. Please remember your son when you look on this point and know that I am proud to be your son." With that, Small Foot stood and looked into the climbing sun, feeling the wind at his back and knowing that another day was fast approaching.

CHAPTER 6

Long before he was ready to get out of bed, Mike heard the wind blowing. He lay quietly under the covers and thought about the dream he had had. It seemed so real! And it made him feel so badly for the young Small Foot and his family. "Times were much different then, and yet, they must have loved and respected one another just like we do today," Mike thought. "How sad it must be to lose a loved one to a freak accident." Mike's thoughts then wandered to the spear point. "Interesting how proud I was to find this," he mused, "and yet, it was the source of great respect and pride in Small Foot's family too. How can I possibly use it to show off?" His thoughts continued in this vein for the next several hours, even after he had gotten out of bed and headed for school. Mike couldn't wait for his father to come home from work that night so he could tell him about his dream and thoughts.

When his father finally came through the door, Mike said, "Dad, I have to talk to you. I think you may find what I say strange, but nevertheless it is important that we have a talk." His dad said, "Right after we have supper, you and I can sit down and chew the fat. What is it you want to talk about?" But Mike answered, "Wait until we have our talk. I have to tell you a story and then I want to explain my feelings about it."

Some hours later after supper was finished and the dishes were done and put away, Mike's dad said, "Well, Mike, if you want to have a talk, now is the time to do it before I get tired and go to bed." They wandered into the den and shut the door. Mike then lay the beautiful spear point on his dad's desk and said, "Dad. Please don't think that I am nuts, but I want to return this point to the place I found it. But, before you say anything, let me tell you a story." He proceeded then to tell his dad the dream he had the previous night about Small Foot and his family. His father sat quietly and only listened. When the story ended and Mike had described how Small Foot had overcome the utter sadness he had experienced and then looked forward to the future, Mike ended with, "This dream has had an amazing effect on me; I think I am beginning to understand that life is much more complicated than I had ever believed or knew. It seems that all of us have to work hard to understand that and, unless we do, so much will be wasted. I want to return this point to the site where I found it because I believe that Small Foot, or someone just like him, placed it there to honour the memories of his father. It would be irreverent and selfish not to leave it where it was so carefully placed. So, what do you think? Am I nuts?"

Mike's dad smiled and said, "You understand that you have only had a dream? The language spoken as well as your ideas of the hunt and the customs are only your modern interpretation of something that only might have happened. We can never know exactly how things occurred so many years ago—and even if the people of that time actually had the feelings and sensibilities you have described." Mike looked pensive and then explained, "I have thought of nothing else all day, dad, and know that what you say is correct. However, no matter what really happened, nevertheless someone left that point where I found it. I truly believe that whoever did that did it for a reason. My dream is as plausible as any other interpretation and I therefore have to return the point out of respect for whoever placed it there."

Mike's dad stood and placed his arm around the thin shoulders of his son and murmured, "Son, you have learned a life's lesson and I am proud that you have. You are well on your way to becoming a man. Of course I will take you back to the site by the river."

On Saturday, Mike and his dad climbed back into the VW and headed out of town. When they drove over the river on the bridge, Mike marvelled at the beauty of the location. The grassy meadow near the large cottonwood trees near the river stood out in the sunlight. Looking above the meadow at the top of the bluff where he had found the point, Mike held his breath. Taking the point once again into his hand, he admired the beauty and artistic design, and the craftsmanship that had formed something so masterful. He knew that his decision was the right one.

Mike and his dad climbed the steep hill to the top of the bluff and walked slowly to the edge of the blowout where the point had lain for so many years. They looked over the edge of the bluff down at the river and then across the river over the grass covered fields to the horizon. There was never anything so beautiful. Mike knelt and dug a shallow hole near the bone remnants. He placed the beautiful point into the hole and then, looked at his dad and smiled.

As they climbed down the hill to the car, the west wind began to blow gently, and Mike could almost believe that he heard the wind singing a song of thanks.

CPSIA information can be obtained at www.ICGtesting.com
Printed in the USA
LVIW01n2324170317
527597LV00003B/13